CAN CAT

AND

BIRD

BE
FRIENDS
?

For Eun Mi

ISBN 978-0-06-286593-9

The artist used Procreate and Adobe to create the digital illustrations for this book.
Design by Coll Muir and Chelsea C. Donaldson
19 20 21 22 23   SCP   10 9 8 7 6 5 4 3 2 1

❖

First Edition

by
COLL
MUIR

HARPER
An Imprint of HarperCollinsPublishers

Are you a bird?

Yes, I am.

Then I must eat you.

Why?

**Because I am a cat,
and cats eat birds.**

Why do cats eat birds?

**I don't know. It's
always been like that.**

Can't I be your friend instead?

**Oh, I'm not sure about that.
How would a bird make
a good friend for a cat?**

Well, I know a fun box
for a cat to play in.

I love this box!

I know the
highest tree
for a cat to get
stuck in.

This tree is
very tall.

And I know the best car for a cat to hide under.

I agree. This is a fantastic car to hide under.

Okay, Bird. You can be my friend.

Wait a second. How would a cat make a good friend for a bird?

Well, let me think . . .

I know the perfect wire for a bird to sit on.

This is a lovely wire!

I know where there are lots of twigs
for a bird to make a nest with.

These are super sticks!

I know where there are loads of juicy worms for a bird to eat.

These worms are totally tasty!

Okay, Bird,
we can be friends.

But friends do things
together, don't they,
Cat?

Yes.

Well, I don't like playing
in boxes, getting stuck
up in high trees, or
hiding under cars.

And I don't like sitting
on wires, making nests,
or eating worms.

You're right. If we're going to be friends, we've got to find something we both like doing.

**So, what do we
both like doing?**

I like
stretching.
Do you?

Not
really.

Do you like licking?

Nope.

Do you like flying?

Of course not.
I'm a cat.

I guess that's it, then. We have nothing in common. We can't be friends!

Oh well. I think I'll just go home.
I've got a painting to finish.

PAINTING?!

I love painting!

I love painting, too!